Jumble the Puppy

Written by Antony Lishak
Illustrated by Jan Smith

Heinemann

Chapter 1

As soon as Dan learned to talk, he began to beg his parents to get him a puppy. First he would try his mum.

'Please, Mum, can we get a puppy? I promise I'll look after it and take it for walks. It won't be any trouble,' said Dan.

'Dogs take a lot of looking after,' said Mum, 'and anyway, I don't want a puppy digging up the garden, now that I've got it looking nice.'

Then Dan would try his dad.

'PLEASE, Dad, can we get a puppy?' begged Dan. 'I'll make sure it doesn't dig up the garden and I'll buy all its food out of my own pocket money.'

'Dogs take a lot of looking after,' said Dad, 'and anyway, we haven't got space in the house for a lively puppy.'

Every birthday and every
Christmas, Dan hoped to find a
puppy waiting for him in the hall.
There were always lots of super
presents but no puppy. Dan began to
think he would never get one.

Then when he was seven, his
parents gave in and bought him
Jumble – a furry, black and white
puppy. He had floppy ears and a
very waggy tail. Dan adored him.

Each day, before and after school,
Dan and Jumble would have great
fun playing together. At night,
Jumble would creep upstairs and
sleep under Dan's bed, even though
he had his own bed in the kitchen.

As long as Dan was there, Jumble was happy, but when Dan was at school, Jumble was very lonely. One day, he wanted Mum to play with him, but she was busy at her computer.

So Jumble played a game in the curtains, pretending Dan was hiding in them. Mum was cross when she saw the big holes in the curtains, so she sent Jumble out into the garden.

Jumble wanted Mum to run round the garden with him like Dan did, but she was still busy. So Jumble played a game with the washing on the line, then he dug up the grass, pretending to look for a lost bone.

Mum was very cross when she saw the big holes in the lawn.

As soon as Dan came home from school, Jumble was happy, but Mum wasn't!

'That dog's driving me mad!' she said to her husband, after Dan had gone to bed. 'I can't cope.'

'What's he done this time?' asked Dad.

'This!' she said, pointing at the torn curtains.

'Oh no!' said Dad.

'But that's not all!' said Mum, and she went to get the washing basket.

One by one, she held up the
clothes that Jumble had pulled off
the line that morning.

'Oh, no! Not my best shirt!'
groaned Dad. 'And look at my
favourite jumper! It isn't much good
with only one sleeve.'

'Look what he's done to my
knickers!' said Mum, holding up a
pair of shredded knickers.

Mum put the clothes back into the basket and flopped down on to the couch.

'It's no good,' she said. 'I just can't cope with Jumble.'

'Perhaps he could stay in a kennel in the garden while Dan is at school,' suggested Dad.

'Don't even think about it,' said Mum, wearily. 'I haven't shown you the mess he's made of the lawn. It looks like a building site – holes everywhere!'

Dad went to look for Jumble in the kitchen, but he wasn't there.

'Humph!' said Dad, as he climbed the stairs and peeped into Dan's bedroom. Dan was sound asleep and so was Jumble. He was under Dan's bed, snoring quietly.

Dad looked at Jumble. He looked so gentle. It was hard to believe it was the same dog who had caused so much damage.

Dad came downstairs and sat
back in his chair. He picked up
the newspaper.

'I suppose we'll have to arrange
for someone else to look after him,
until he's past the mad puppy stage,'
said Dad. He stared at his wife
through the hole Jumble had made in
the newspaper. 'But it won't be easy
telling Dan.'

Chapter 2

The next day was Saturday and Dan and Jumble were looking forward to their favourite outing of the week. Every Saturday after tea, Dad took them to Smugglers Wood. It was a patch of woodland not far from their house. Dan and Jumble loved to search there for buried treasure.

Dad decided it would be easier to tell Dan about their plans for Jumble when they got to Smugglers Wood.

Dan was standing by the front door and Jumble was charging up and down the hall.

'Come on, Dad. Jumble and I are ready.'

'I'm just getting my boots,' said Dad. And he bent down to get his boots from the cupboard under the stairs.

Jumble couldn't wait any longer. Spinning with excitement, he jumped up at Dan. Dan watched in horror as Jumble's waggly tail swept a vase of flowers crashing to the floor.

For a moment, Dan thought
nobody had seen what happened as
Dad still had his head in the
cupboard. Then he heard
Mum's shriek.

'That really does it. That dog will
have to ....'

But Dan didn't hear what Mum
said because Jumble was so startled
by Mum's cry that he backed
quickly away.

He bumped into Dad, who was coming out of the cupboard backwards. Dad toppled head first into the cupboard.

'Ow!' Dad yelled. Then there was a scraping sound and another even louder 'Ow!' as a broom in the cupboard fell crashing down on Dad's head.

Dan decided it was time to get Jumble out of the way. 'We'll wait for you by the gate,' he called to Dad, as he and Jumble ran from the house.

By the time they got to Smugglers
Wood, Dad had almost stopped
complaining about Jumble. Dan
noticed a rather large bump on Dad's
head but he thought it would be a
good idea not to mention it.

Dan let Jumble off the lead as
soon as they got to the woods.
Smugglers Wood had lots of great
places where pirates could have
hidden their treasure. Dan was sure
that if he and Jumble looked hard
enough, they would find some
pirates' gold.

Since he and Jumble had started playing the treasure hunt game, Dan had found silver bottle tops and shiny sweet wrappers. Jumble was good at nosing round in the undergrowth and finding 'treasure'. Dan kept all the treasure they found in a box under his bed.

Once last year, he had found a coin he thought was old and going to be worth lots of money. But when they got home and Dad washed off the mud, they saw that the coin was shiny and quite new.

Dad said, 'I don't think there were many pirates round a few years ago.'

When Dan woke up the next morning, he had found a bag of gold coins on his pillow with a card from his dad. Inside it said, *"Here's the treasure I bought with the treasure you found yesterday!"*

It may not have been real treasure but it was the tastiest! After Dan had eaten all the chocolate coins, he put the gold wrappers in the box under his bed.

In the middle of Smugglers Wood, Dan and Jumble set off on their latest search. They went straight to the river that flowed through the woods.

'Look how much water there is,' Dan said to Jumble. 'It must have been raining a lot to make the river that deep.' Jumble barked twice, as if to say he agreed with every word Dan said.

'Come on, Jumble. Let's go and look by the giant oak,' called Dan. Then Dan heard Dad calling him.

'Dan! Dan! There's something I want to talk to you about.'

'Don't worry, Dad. We won't play near the river,' Dan shouted back.

'It's about Jumble,' said Dad, as he walked up to Dan.

'I won't let Jumble go near the river either,' said Dan.

'It's not about the river,' said Dad. 'It's about Jumble. Your mother and I have decided that we just can't keep him. He gets into too much mischief when you're at school.'

'What do you mean?' asked Dan, looking puzzled.

'Well, he's not really a suitable dog for us. We're going to have to find him another home.'

'But why?' asked Dan, his eyes filling with tears.

'He's such trouble in the house, Dan,' said Dad. 'Every day he breaks or spoils something. It's like having a monster in the house.'

'Jumble is NOT a monster!' cried Dan. 'He's my best friend and if you send him away, I'll run away too.'

Dan ran off to join Jumble. Dad watched his son throwing his arms round the dog.

Chapter 3

Dad sat down on a log by the river, feeling sad for Dan. Jumble would have to go. Dad felt he had no choice. 'Dan will get used to the idea, eventually,' thought Dad. 'And if Jumble can be trained, then maybe, one day, he can come back to live with us.'

Dad threw a stick into the swirling river and watched it being tossed and flipped by the fast flowing water.

Meanwhile, Dan sat down under the giant oak hugging Jumble. 'I won't ever let them take you away,' he told the dog. Jumble whined sadly and licked the tears from Dan's unhappy face. 'I'll say that you'll promise never to break anything again,' said Dan, and Jumble barked in agreement. 'I'll say that from now on you'll stay in my room all the time and if you break anything of mine, I won't mind,' said Dan.

Jumble put his head on one side, as if he was listening very carefully. Dan was cheering up. As soon as Jumble saw a smile on Dan's face, he leaped round and started searching for treasure. 'That's right, Jumble,' said Dan. 'I bet we'll find some real treasure today.'

Dad stood up from the log to see where Dan and Jumble had gone. He was pleased to see them both playing the treasure hunt game. 'Perhaps Dan understands why Jumble must go,' thought Dad. 'And maybe we could get him a present of some sort – to make up for not having the dog. He's always going on about some kind of bike. Yes, that's it! We'll get him a bike and he'll soon forget about Jumble.'

Dan and Jumble ran round the wood, looking for treasure. They looked under stones and in hollow logs. They found some tin foil which Dan put in his pocket, but they didn't find a single coin.

'No treasure this time, boy,' said Dan, ruffling the fur between Jumble's ears. We'd better get back to Dad. He'll be waiting for us.'

Jumble had one last search in a pile of leaves and then he rushed over to join Dan.

When they got back to the log where Dad had been waiting, there was no sign of him.

'Dad? Dad?' called Dan. 'Where are you?' There was no reply. Dan called again, 'Dad? Dad?' shouting at the top of his voice. There was still no answer.

Dan listened as hard as he could, but all he could hear was the sound of the rushing river.

Then Jumble started to bark.

'Be quiet, Jumble. I'm trying to listen for Dad!' But Jumble went on barking. He was running round and round in circles, at the top of the river bank.

Dan called to him. 'Stop it, Jumble! Don't be naughty. I've got to listen for Dad.' But Jumble would not stop. He barked all the louder. Dan went over to him. Then he saw what was making Jumble bark so madly.

At the bottom of the river bank, beside the flowing water, was Dad.

'Dad! what are you doing down there?' asked Dan. 'I thought you always told us it was dangerous to go near the river!'

'Get some help, Dan!' called Dad.
'I've hurt my ankle and I can't move!'
'Don't worry, Dad,' he called.
'I'll go and tell Mum. I'll be as quick
as I can. Come on, Jumble! We've got
to get help.'

Dan began to run in the direction
of the house. Then he realised that
Jumble was not with him. He turned
round to see Jumble sitting at the top
of the river bank.

'Come on, Jumble! This is important!' yelled Dan. But Jumble would not move.

'Bad dog!' said Dan, crossly. 'Maybe Mum and Dad are right. Maybe you are too naughty.'

With that, Dan turned away and ran off to his house.

Chapter 4

So Dan didn't see Jumble climbing down the slippery, steep river bank. He didn't see Jumble walk carefully over to Dad and gently nuzzle his hand. For a long time Jumble lay quietly by Dad.

The last bits of light disappeared from the sky and it was pitch black.

Suddenly Jumble got to his feet and began to bark.

'Quiet, Jumble, there's a good boy,' whispered Dad.

But Jumble continued to bark.

Dad saw a light at the top of the bank and Jumble barked even louder. Then Dad heard a voice.

'Are you all right down there?'

Before long, an ambulance man was making his way along the river bank to where Dad lay.

'You're a very lucky guy,' said the man. 'We didn't know how we were going to find you. We couldn't hear anything above the noise of the river, but when your dog barked, we knew we'd found you.'

Then the ambulance man looked at Dad's ankle.

'Looks like a break,' he said. 'Don't worry, we'll have you out of here in no time.'

Jumble stayed close to Dad.

'You've got a fine dog there,' said the man. He's really looking after you.'

'I know, said Dad. 'He found me in the first place. And he's kept me warm ever since. It's been like having a hot water bottle.'

'He looks like he's only a puppy,' said the man. 'You certainly owe him a lot.'

'Actually, he's my son's dog. To tell you the truth, he's a bit of a monster,' said Dad.

'Who is?' asked the ambulance man, rather surprised. 'Your son?'

'No, the dog!' said Dad. 'He's a bit of a wrecker! You should see what he can do to a line of washing!'

'Well, I'd be proud of him if he was my dog,' said the man. 'He's done you a big favour tonight.'

The ambulance man gave Jumble a pat on the back. Jumble licked the man's face and whimpered in delight. He wagged his tail so hard against the man's leg, that it sounded like a drum being struck by a giant.

'He's a friendly little thing, isn't he? He must be such fun to have round.'

Dad smiled faintly.

'Here I come,' called a voice from above. Slowly, another ambulance man brought a stretcher for Dad. The men strapped him in.

'Okay, let's go!' they said.

Slowly, the men carried Dad up to the top of the bank. Jumble scrambled up the river bank to be there to greet him.

Mum was waiting at the top of the bank.

'Whatever happened?' she asked.

'Well,' said Dad, 'I feel a bit silly. I saw something gold and shiny sticking out of the river bank and I tried to pull it out. I leaned over a bit too far and I slipped.'

'You found some buried treasure?' asked Dan, excitedly.

'Not exactly,' said Dad. And he felt for something in his pocket. He stuck his hand out from under the blanket. In his hand was a golden crisp packet. 'This is the buried treasure,' he said, sheepishly.

Dan took the crisp packet. 'I'll put it with all the other treasure, in the box under my bed,' he said.

'Come on, mate. The ambulance
is waiting to take you to hospital.'
The men carefully lifted the stretcher.

'Never mind, Dan,' said Dad.
'There will be plenty of time for you
and Jumble to search for real buried
treasure. And maybe after a few
puppy-training classes he might even
learn to behave himself in the
house too.'

'Does that mean Jumble can stay?' asked Dan, excitedly.

'What do YOU think?' asked Dad, smiling up at his wife.

'How could we possibly let him go?' Mum said. 'He's a hero!'

About the author
Antony Lishak

When I was a child my best friend was a dog called Rusty. When he was a pup he would bite off our door handles, chew up our carpet, howl like a wolf and steal all my chocolates. But I still loved him. Happily, so did my parents.

He grew up to be so clever that I used to think he was really a human dressed as a dog. I even remember searching for a zip on his belly!

I think he would have howled with delight to know that I had written a story that was inspired by him.

About the illustrator

Jan Smith

I became an artist
because I wanted to
draw. I've always loved
drawing and making up characters.
I soon learned though that you need to
be able to draw things as they really
are, before you can turn them into
something funny!

When I'm drawing a character and
I can't get the expression right, I put
a mirror on my desk and 'pull a face'
so that I can copy it. It might seem
strange, but it works!

If the picture really goes wrong,
I'll leave it and go back later –
maybe after I've been shopping!
I love my job.